Glamsters

For my Glameditor, Alessandra Balzer
—E.C.K.

First Edition
1 0 9 8 7 6 5 4 3 2 1
Printed in Singapore
Reinforced binding
ISBN 978-1-4231-1148-1
Library of Congress Cataloging-in-Publication Data on file.
Visit www.hyperionbooksforchildren.com

For all the homeless in the world,
and for everyone big-hearted enough
to give someone a family
—J.U.

Glamsters

written by Elizabeth Cody Kimmel
illustrated by Jackie Urbanovic

Hyperion Books for Children
New York
An Imprint of Disney Book Group

BOOKS
HAMSTER
DIGES

Harriet the Hamster was vexed.

Between the neon sign blinking HAMSTER WORLD and her sister Patricia's snores, she was wide awake. Hamster World was having its huge annual sale in the morning. It was the hamsters' big chance to be adopted, and she had to get her beauty sleep.

Harriet decided to read some of the magazine pages the assistant store manager had used to line their cage. Sometimes she got lucky and found a whole issue of *Nuts and Seeds Weekly* or *Hamsters Digest*. She loved reading the pages of *Hamsters at Home*, filled with photos of hamsters in their luxurious new homes.

"What if I'm never chosen?" Harriet murmured. "No one ever seems to notice Patricia and me."

Patricia gave a little snore and rolled over. Harriet's eye was caught by the page Patricia had been lying on.

Not Getting Noticed? Now YOU can go from Hamster to Glamster!

“Well, here is something interesting!” Harriet said.

Harriet scanned the article, and her eyes grew wide. There were pictures of Glamsters everywhere. Their fur was sleek and shiny. They wore fancy, glittering shoes and enormous, white-rimmed sunglasses.

I bet if I looked like *that*, I'd be noticed in record time, Harriet thought. All she had to do was follow a few simple steps.

Harriet took the five-minute "Rate your Glamster Potential" quiz. She chose her signature colors, and filled out a questionnaire called "Is Your Coat Dazzling or Dull?"

She created her own version of their High Gloss–and–Glo Fur Volumizer, using carrot juice, water, and essence of sesame-seed husk. She rubbed the potion over every inch of her fur, just as the article said.

“Why, I feel tingly and sleek already!” Harriet declared. Patricia continued to snore away.

Harriet followed the instructions under “Create Your Unique Look” and made a glamorous hat. She used a wrapper from a Life Savers Tropical Fruits roll to give it an exotic, rainbow look.

"I can practically feel the glamour oozing out of me!

"What shall I do next?"

Harriet looked at Patricia.
Then she knew exactly what to do.

Using slivers of leftover seed packaging, Harriet fashioned Patricia a lovely set of whisker extensions, and glued them into place with celery paste. They looked so nice, she made another set for herself.

A few minutes later, Patricia woke up. When she saw Harriet, she began to scream. She screamed so high and so loud that Harriet began to scream too.

"What is it, Patricia?" Harriet cried.

"Harriet?" whispered Patricia.

"Of course it's Harriet!" Harriet answered. "Who else would I be?"

"I was dreaming about space aliens. I thought you were one of them."

Harriet laughed. "It's the new me, Patricia! I've transformed myself."

And she gave a little twirl. “Ta-da!” Harriet announced. “I’m a Glamster!”

Patricia just stared.

"Darling, it's the key to getting us noticed!"

Patricia shook her head. "Oh, Harriet. I don't know what to say."

"That's all right. You're my sister and I love you. We'll give *you* a makeover too!"

Patricia looked Harriet up and down. "Well . . ."

"I know! Don't you just love it? I started with High Gloss–and–Glo Fur Volumizer as my signature look. And, given a little more time, I think I can produce a two-tone claw polish that will—"

"But, Harriet," Patricia interrupted, "have you actually looked at yourself?"

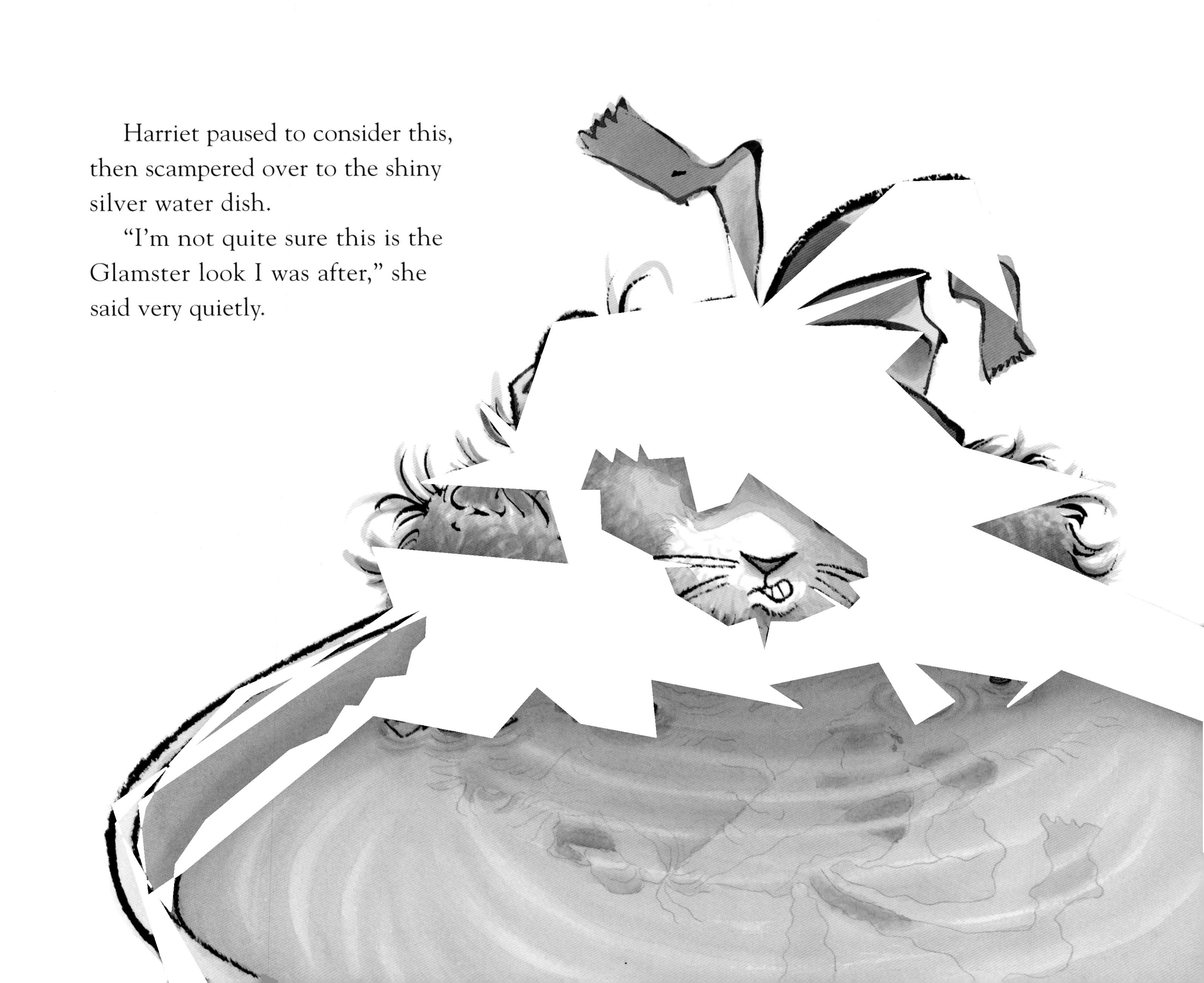

Harriet paused to consider this, then scampered over to the shiny silver water dish.

"I'm not quite sure this is the Glamster look I was after," she said very quietly.

Patricia put a paw around her sister.

Overhead, the lights began coming on. Hamster World was opening for business.

Harriet buried her face in Patricia's soft fur. "What was I thinking?" Harriet moaned. "No one will want me now. I'm FrankenHamster!"

"Harriet," Patricia said.

"Some nice little girl is going to take you home, and I'll be stuck here, and we'll never see each other again!" Harriet wailed.

"Harriet," Patricia repeated.

"We've always been together," Harriet howled. "That's all that really matters, and now it's too late!"

“Harriet, snap out of it!” Patricia picked up Harriet and tossed her into the water bowl.

Harriet spluttered and swam until Patricia reached in and hauled her out.

"Well, that's definitely an improvement," Patricia said.

"The magazine"—Harriet paused between words to let her teeth chatter—"said we needed to be Glamsters to get noticed. And today is the sale!"

Patricia pulled a flannel scrap out of the bed pile and began toweling Harriet off.

"All of our brothers and sisters got homes," Patricia said.

"Yes," Harriet sniffed.

"And they weren't Glamsters," Patricia added.

"No," Harriet snuffled.

"Well, then," Patricia said, giving Harriet's back another brisk rub. "You don't look like FrankenHamster anymore. The family resemblance is back."

Harriet noticed a little girl a few feet away, watching them closely.

"Really, Harriet, you mustn't worry yourself so," Patricia chattered, still rubbing Harriet with the towel.

Harriet stood stock-still. The little girl walked over to the cage. She looked at Harriet. She looked at Patricia. Then she smiled.

"Patricia," Harriet whispered, "I think we're being chosen."

Patricia nodded.

"How do I look?" Harriet asked.

Patricia leaned in close to her ear. “You look,” she whispered, “like you.” Harriet put her hat back on her head, and beamed.